The Lust Bunny

Helen Walton

Walton House Publishing

Contents

A Short Story

♥

THIS WAS IT. TIME for me to make it or break it. My last chance to prove to my family I'd become a 'real' actress, as they referred to it. To them, acting in commercials wasn't real acting and I shouldn't call myself an actress. Bunch of know-it-alls. I wasn't close to my family for this reason. Not spending time with them this Easter holiday was as easy as accepting this small part in a film.

My phone buzzed with a message from my best friend and roommate, Emily.

Break a leg.

About to tap back a reply, another message beeped through the phone.

My bestie is about to be famous!

I grinned. At least I had her support. Even if she complained about my over-the-top costume parties. So did my other roomie, Jake. No matter how much they said they didn't enjoy dressing up for parties, they both went to them because they loved me. If only my family showed me the same unconditional love.

I was a real actress. About to be in a movie. Even if I only had a small supporting part, at least this role was in a movie, and my family could shove their not-a-real actress where the sun doesn't shine.

The sun was, in fact, shining. The weather was perfect, sitting in the mid-twenties. I was about to spend Easter and the next few weeks on an island. Louve Island. Who named an island that? Whoever it was must have watched the Love Boat when they were younger. Grammy mentioned the show to me when I said I was coming here. It'd been her favorite show for many years.

She was the one family member who supported me and my career choice. Perhaps because she'd raised me while Mom and Dad worked hard as attorneys, and I was a late surprise child. One they didn't, for the most part, seem to want. My older brothers were off at college when I appeared, so it was no wonder we weren't close.

The island drew nearer. A little oasis away from my life. A place I'd act like anyone else because no one knew me there and would tell me I wasn't an actress The ferry chugged into port and docked at the jetty. I stood on shaky sea legs and made my way off the boat, dragging my suitcase behind me. As I stepped onto the gangplank, I staggered against the guardrail, almost toppling into the sloshing water underneath.

"Easy there," a man said, grabbing hold of my upper arm and steadying me.

"Sorry," I stammered.

"Not a problem," he said.

My reflection shone back at me in his mirrored glasses. He released me and walked down the gangplank with a stride I ogled.

I recognized his swagger from somewhere. But where?

As he approached the jetty, a woman rushed forward, screaming. *What the hell?* She bounced up and down on her toes, sending her blonde hair flying around her face. The man smiled, slid his sunglasses off his face, and said something I couldn't hear, then walked away, leaving the woman gazing after him with hearts in her eyes. If such a thing was possible. The woman followed behind him at a restrained distance. He turned and winked over his shoulder. She almost swooned to the ground. I giggled to myself and followed behind the pair. More women rushed the man.

It hit me. He was Conrad Saint James, a famous actor. Also, the star of the movie. How hadn't I recognized him? His outfit of a palm tree shirt, beige cargo shorts, and flip-flops had disguised him. He looked every bit like a tourist instead of his usual dark jeans and tight t-shirt, and a leather jacket if the weather was cool. A man I hadn't spotted before dressed in all black stepped forward and ushered the women away. Conrad waved at them, looking disappointed as his bodyguard stepped in.

I pursed my lips. Famous actors boasted the life. Major roles in films. Fans. Bodyguards. Enough money to buy whatever clothes they wanted while on location. A famous actor's life was what I longed for. Everything Conrad had, I wanted. This role here would be an enormous step in my path to my goal. I had one scene opposite Conrad where I'd act with him. My limbs tingled with excitement. If I did the role well, then he'd ask for me again. That was my hope anyway.

Conrad and his bodyguard disappeared into the reception building. I followed, not in the stalker fan way, but because I needed to check in too. The bodyguard threw me an appraising stare, but when I didn't rush his charge, he turned back to Conrad. The woman behind the counter shook in excitement to serve the famous actor. I nibbled my lip to stop myself from laughing at how flustered she became. Conrad patted her hand as she handed the key to his bungalow. Her eyelids flew open. The touch meant nothing to Conrad. He walked past me without even sparing me a glance.

So much for being noticed by him.

At least he wasn't ignoring my acting skills. Merely my presence. I suppose, when you were famous, it would be easy to ignore people who didn't swoon over you. The door closed behind him and his bodyguard.

"Can I help you?" the woman asked.

I stepped forward. "Hi, yes, I have a bungalow booked."

"Sure, what name is it under?"

"Natalie Katz."

She tapped away on the computer. "Here you are. You're booked into bungalow number eight. I hope you enjoy your stay."

"Thanks." I picked up the key and the map she slid across the counter.

"You're welcome. If you have questions, please don't hesitate to come back and ask. I'm Claire."

"Will do. There aren't any Easter Bunnies about to jump out at me, are there?"

Claire battled with a smile. "No. We don't celebrate traditional holidays on the island."

"Good." I nodded, glad I wouldn't have Easter rubbed in my face, making me feel guilty for not spending the time with my family.

Outside, a pleasant breeze blew across the ocean and caressed my hair. Tickles danced along my neck, and I almost laughed, imagining a boyfriend, which I didn't have, kissing the back of my neck. My family scared most men. Perhaps because most men I dated were bad boys with attitudes and sometimes a record to go with it. I couldn't help the way their 'I'm sexy and don't give a shit' attitude turned me on. Mom said I was a magnet for assholes. She didn't understand the whole bad boy appeal. Leather jackets, motorbikes, tattoos... yum.

As I daydreamed of tattoos, Conrad stood on the beach and stripped off his hideous shirt. His back was to me, which was a good and a bad thing because his back had a tattoo. One which drew my gaze and made me want to follow the lines with my tongue.

I sighed and dragged my eyes to the path before me. Lusting after Conrad Saint James was a given. He was hot. Dark hair. Dark eyes. Everything about him was dark and mysterious and the reason women swooned after him.

I lifted the map and followed the boardwalk to my designated bungalow. The trek was pleasant, with a bunch of green plants, butterflies, and birds flapping between the leaves. I found the charming bungalow and let myself in. The interior was like an extension of the outside. Plants were in various places around the room. They'd decorated everything in a bright and airy way, making my lungs ease with each breath. I dragged my suitcase to the bedroom, unpacked my belongings, and bounced on the side of the bed.

Not too soft and not too hard. Just right. I giggled. I'm Goldilocks. Three big, bad bears are going to bust in my door and tell me to get out.

I jumped up and acted out the scene, pretending I was Goldilocks and flabbergasted at three bears finding me in their bed. After I'd played out my brief scene, I flopped face-first onto the bed and laughed into the pillow. Acting was so much fun. Why didn't any of my family understand how good it was to escape reality and pretend you were someone else?

My phone beeped. I tapped the smartwatch and turned off the notification. Time to meet the cast.

Conrad stood next to the director as he greeted everyone and gave us all a big spiel that breezed in one ear, whizzed around my head, then got lost. I endeavored to concentrate. I did, but this was way too exciting. My first film role.

Filming didn't start until Tuesday, so those of us who'd arrived on the island early had time to ourselves to either party with fellow cast members, rehearse our lines, or frequent the local nightlife. I rushed back to my bungalow, eager to check out the local bar, which I'd already researched on the website. The nightlife looked way too good to pass up. One of my poor qualities. I liked bars. And men.

I showered in the most deluxe shower I'd ever used. An enormous head rained water down on me as I scrubbed my hair, shaved my legs, because you never knew when you'd get lucky, and used the luxurious body wash in the welcome package. A citrus and coconut tang filled the air, adding to the holiday island experience. The shower was heaven and leaving it was a chore, but I promised I'd be back every day, maybe multiple times a day, with how good the water pelted my body.

My stomach gurgled. I planned to grab a quick bite and dine at the bar, which was in the same building as the restaurant, so I assumed they served meals at the bar, too. As I dressed in my skimpy denim skirt and halter-neck white top, I sang at the top of my lungs. I might be a terrible singer, but I didn't let my off-key notes stop me from having fun. Sliding on my strappy sandals, I grabbed the bungalow key and locked the door.

Tip tapping along the boardwalk, I hummed out of tune.

The bodyguard I'd seen with Conrad stepped ahead of me and blocked my path. "Excuse me, miss."

"Um." I faltered to a stop.

"We'll be a moment."

I attempted to peer past the bodyguard's massive shoulders, but he was huge, and, with the dimming light of the approaching night, his big black suit was a shadow that wouldn't move. After a few minutes, he stepped aside and walked down the boardwalk. I followed behind him since I assumed Conrad was heading toward the bar, too. As my heels clicked, I hummed the offbeat tune again. The bodyguard flicked a glance over his shoulder, frowned, then turned back around. I stopped humming, feeling like my father had chastised me yet again.

With no sound coming from me, every other noise petered in. The music up ahead.

Laughter. Clinking glasses. Chatter. This was what I wanted. I hurried my pace, but with the immovable brick of the bodyguard in front of me, I wouldn't get there any quicker. Patience was never my strong suit. As soon as we stepped off the boardwalk, I rushed around the bodyguard and caught sight of Conrad, which almost made me stumble. He'd dressed in designer jeans, hugging his tight buttocks and lean hips. A black t-shirt, simple, yet effective in highlighting his muscular biceps.

Mmm, arm porn.

I was an absolute sucker for well-toned arms.

With the conscious knowledge the bodyguard would once again get between me and Conrad if I stared much longer, I breezed on past like he wasn't a famous actor or a sexy man who made my thighs tremble.

I opened the door and rushed inside the bar. People crowded the space, so I squeezed my way through the throng to get to the bar and between two men at the counter. When I caught the eye of the bartender, I waved him over. He grinned and sauntered over to me.

"What'll it be?" he asked.

"Martini," I said. "Do you serve meals in here?"

He slapped a menu on the bar. Hooray for my stomach. I scanned the list while he made my cocktail. No way I'd wait to order with this many people here. By the time he returned, I'd already settled on a serving of deep-fried flaming shrimp. I grabbed the flashing disk that would let me see when my order was ready and walked through the throng of people to a dark corner where I'd sit back and observe the goings on.

Before too long, my disk flashed, and I was back at the bar collecting my shrimp. Luck flowed my way when a man slid off the bar stool and I could sit on it and eat at the bar. I popped the tiny parcels of shrimp in my mouth. Eat bite grew hotter until I drained my martini and ordered another.

"Here you go, miss," the bartender said, placing my glass on the counter. "Those shrimp sure pack a punch, don't they?"

"They do, and so does the sauce." I dipped another shrimp into the spicy sauce. "They're delicious though."

"Tell me about it. I get a takeaway pack almost every night. Perks of the job."

"I'll be getting them every day while I'm here."

Conrad's bodyguard stepped up to the bar and ordered drinks. I peeked around him, not finding Conrad next to the bodyguard, which was a tad strange, but with nothing better to do, I returned to devouring my shrimp.

"Excuse me?" a man asked.

"Yes?" I turned my focus from the food and stared into the hopeful expression of a man with baby blue eyes and soft blond hair. Nothing about him was anything like my type. He was cute, though.

"Would you like to dance?"

"Sure, why not?" I wiped my mouth on a napkin, sipped the rest of my drink, and let him lead me to the dance floor where people were getting their groove on to the latest hits.

We shimmied and shook our booties to the music. The man was cute and respectful while we danced. And not my type. I needed a man to grab me. Haul me close and whisper dirty words in my ear. I thanked him for the dance and turned, almost colliding with Conrad Saint James. He steadied me by placing his hands on my hips. Tiny shivers of desire danced over my skin. I licked my lips and peered into his dark eyes.

"Sorry," I said.

"No problem."

He didn't let go, and we both stood there staring at each other in a hypnotic, lustful kind of trance. A woman bumped into me from behind and shoved me further into Conrad's embrace. He ran his hands around my back and hauled me against his body. I shivered with desire. He rocked us into a grinding dance to the throbbing music.

One hand slid up my bare back and toyed with the ties of my halter-neck top.

He leaned in and whispered in my ear, "If I untie these, will I find a bra underneath?"

Hello, bad boy. I was putty in his hands.

"Only one way to find out," I said.

He sank his mouth to my shoulder. "I have a serious thing for bare shoulders."

"I might use that against you."

He raised his head. "Do you know who I am?"

"Of course. But I meant it in a personal way, not an 'I'll tell the newspapers way'."

He threw his head back and laughed.

"You're funny and hot. How about an island fling?"

"Do you think I'm easy?" I fluttered my eyelashes.

"Knowing my luck, the only woman here I want isn't into me." He dipped his chin and gave me puppy dog eyes.

I giggled. "Conrad Saint James, there isn't a woman who wouldn't be into you."

"Not true. My brother's girlfriend, Olive Sanchez, isn't into me."

"Well, I should hope not. That'd be awkward."

"Neither is her sister Hazel." He pouted his bottom lip. "See, there are lots of women not into me."

"Oh, woe is me. I'm rich, and famous, handsome too, yet not every woman on the planet wants me."

"See, you get me, wild thing with your curly hair."

"Do you like curls, too?" I lifted an eyebrow.

"Yes, above all brunettes. Everyone thinks blondes have more fun, but brunettes are dirtier in bed."

I fought the laughter building in my chest, but I couldn't hold it back and burst out laughing.

"I guess it takes one to know one."

"It does. So my bungalow or yours?"

"Neither."

I wouldn't risk my valuable acting break with a quick fling with the lead actor. As tempting as Conrad was, being another notch on his bedpost, for I was sure that's all I'd be, I needed this role and movie to work out. I might like men, but I wouldn't sleep my way to a career.

"No?"

"No."

"Ah, well, perhaps it's for the best. I might become besotted with you if I found out how wild you are in bed."

I laughed again. "You're tempting me."

"But not enough?"

I shook my head.

"Okay." He stopped swaying us to the song.

Every nerve in my body screamed to take him to bed, but I dropped my arms from his body where I'd been clinging onto his thick biceps. My palms were warm and tingling, as though they'd come alive from touching him.

"Thank you for the dance." He dipped his head and brushed his lips over my mouth.

Sparks of desire shot through my lips. I opened my mouth and met the probing tip of his tongue sweeping across my lips. He swept inside, taking me with a demanding kiss that made my knees shake. I might kiss Conrad forever. He was the best kisser I'd ever had, but I shouldn't be kissing him, of all people. As I went to end the kiss, he did so first. He touched a hand to his lips. I understood how he felt. My mouth tingled with awareness, as did the rest of my body.

"Crap," I muttered under my breath. *How would I say no now?*

His tongue darted out to his plump lips, then he lifted his palm to scrub his mouth. From turned on to humiliated in a second. How embarrassing he wanted to scrub our kiss from his mouth. Heat flooded my cheeks. I turned to leave.

"Wait!"

"What?" I faced him.

"Did you eat shellfish?"

He rubbed his lips again. Had they grown? Were they swelling? No, no, no.

"Ah, I ate prawns."

"I'm allergic."

"Shit, what do we do?" I glanced around wildly, looking for something, anything, but I didn't comprehend what.

He grabbed my arm. I snapped my gaze to his. Red blotches surrounded his lips.

"Relax," he said, but his voice came out slurred or like he possessed a lisp. "I need an antihistamine."

If his mouth swelled, then would he stop breathing too? I grabbed his arm and tugged him off the dance floor. People stared. Of course, they did. He was Conrad freaking Saint James. They'd perhaps stared while we'd been dancing and kissing, and I'd been too busy swooning in his arms to notice.

"Is there even a chemist here on the island?" I screamed.

Conrad laughed and waved a hand at me while his eyes bulged in his head and his breathing... was he even breathing? Oh my God, I was about to be a murderer. Would they call it murder or manslaughter? Did it matter? My heart raced in my chest. Now what? I was about to have a heart attack.

The bodyguard shoved through the crowd and reached our side as I considered giving Conrad mouth-to-mouth. Except that'd make him worse since I'd still have shellfish on me. He yanked a puffer from his suit pocket and held it up to Conrad's mouth. Conrad sucked in two gulps. Every second was a living nightmare. The bodyguard popped a pill from a packet and Conrad placed it in his mouth and clicked his fingers. A glass of water appeared from somewhere and he sipped the water to swallow the pill. Then he swished a mouthful of water around his mouth and spat into another cup. He kept rinsing his mouth until the water was gone.

"I'm so sorry. I'm so sorry," I rambled.

The bodyguard shot me a filthy glare, then stepped between us. With nothing but a wall of black suit to stare at, I couldn't even see if Conrad was going to be all right. People whispered behind their hands. Some even pointed. The bodyguard was between me and his charge, and he was determined to stay between them. I wasn't getting anywhere. Conrad must be all right, otherwise, they would have rushed him from here and off the island to a hospital. I hung my head and slunk out of the bar.

Tears threatened my eyes as I staggered back to the bungalow. What a catastrophe. How would I act in this movie now when I'd almost killed the leading man?

As the sun rose the next morning, I hoped with everything inside me, the night was a nightmare of my overactive imagination. I longed to hop on the ferry and escape from finding out the awful truth that I'd killed Conrad. There'd been no sirens last night, or police knocking on my bungalow door, but they might put together an investigation first. Who comprehended how these things worked?

If I left, then my chance to act in a movie would disappear. They'd never hire me again if I dipped out at the last minute. I suppose a murder conviction might be a good excuse.

Argh!

I wouldn't know what happened to Conrad unless I went to the cast meeting tomorrow. It was the only way I'd understand for sure.

I'd never eat shellfish again. Or nuts. Is he allergic to those, too? And why wasn't everyone aware he was allergic to shellfish?

Not that it would have stopped me from eating it, because there's no way I would have guessed we'd kiss.

I tugged the sheets over my head. If I hid all day, then I could pretend it was a nightmare. Worst Easter ever, and that was saying something. Was the universe out to get me because I hadn't spent it with my family?

The next morning, I showered under the rain head, but even the pleasurable spray didn't ease my dark mood. Dressing and stepping out of the bungalow, a glorious blue sky greeted me, as did the birds chirping in happiness. I almost screamed at them to shut up.

How did people live with allergic reactions and not tell everyone they met?

Conrad's red lips and face flashed in front of my face. What if he'd died looking horrendous?

I dragged my feet down the boardwalk to the designated meeting area where the film studio had set up large white tents on the beach for the duration of filming. My hand shook as I parted the flap and walked into the largest tent. I slunk around the edge of the tent, hoping no one would notice me or recognize me from the night before last. The director stood at the front of the tent, waving everyone closer. I'd made it here in time for his speech, but a soft buzzing took up precedence in my ears. I scanned the crowd looking for Conrad but couldn't find his distinctive frame anywhere. Sweat built on my skin.

"Thank you everyone for your prompt arrival. I'm so happy to have everyone here for this film," the director said. "We needed to rearrange the filming schedule for today because of an incident with our leading man."

Murmurs rippled through my fellow actors. I pretended to be as astonished as them.

"Conrad is fine. He needs a day or two to get over an allergic reaction, that's all," the director said.

My entire body sagged in relief. Conrad was okay. He'd get over me almost killing him. I should apologize. It was the least I could do, wasn't it? Maybe even a fruit basket? So long as he wasn't allergic to anything else. Better I stick to an apology. At least words wouldn't hurt him.

The director continued speaking, and with my plan in place for an apology, I concentrated on my big acting break. When he'd finished, we all drifted off to our designated areas. Since the schedule had changed, I was to act in a scene today, so I walked to the wardrobe and then makeup. The entire time I worried someone would recognize me as the woman with Conrad last night, but either it was too dark, or people were oblivious to me causing Conrad's allergic episode.

Dressed and waiting in the wings, I ran my lines through my head. When it was my time to shine, I strolled onto the stage as though

I was the star. My lines came effortlessly. I'd always held a perfect retention memory that served me well in school. Another reason my parents disliked my career choice was that I'd always achieved good grades. They'd assumed I'd follow in their footsteps. Well, this woman was making her footsteps across the big screen. Next movie role, I'd be the star. Wait and see.

The scene ran without a problem, and my day was over so fast I'd barely believed I'd acted in my first movie role. I almost skipped to the dressing room tent, then remembered I needed to apologize to Conrad. How would I talk to him when I didn't know which bungalow he was staying in? How would I find out? I suppose I'd look for the place where his fans were congregating, but with his bodyguard on duty, then he wouldn't let a crowd gather.

What to do?

I changed clothes with the other actors wrapping up for the day.

"Did you see Conrad's face?" Sheila, another actress, asked.

The woman standing beside her shook her head.

"No, he wouldn't let anyone see him. He's too afraid to lose his good looks reputation." She laughed.

I hid my scowl behind the rack of clothes. I doubted that was his reason for staying in today. The man had struggled to breathe. If these women witnessed him in the middle of an allergic reaction, then they'd know how bad it'd been at the time.

"I'm going to see him now," Sheila said.

"What makes you think his bodyguard will let you pass?"

Sheila shrugged. "I'm the leading lady. He'd let me in to read lines."

Sneaky idea. I wished I'd been able to say I was the leading lady. She had a good excuse. At least now, I'd follow Sheila and find the bungalow Conrad was staying in. Even if he allowed Sheila in, I'd be able to try my luck at apologizing later. Sheila slipped out of the tent, and I followed at a discreet distance. The good thing about this place was the boardwalks didn't make it seem like you were following someone. There was no other choice but to follow the paths.

Sheila veered off a path at a sign, pointing to bungalow seven. Even easier to pretend I wasn't following her since I was in bungalow eight, I continued along the path, pretending I was walking to my bungalow. At the last second, I doubled back and observed her knock on Conrad's door. The brawny bodyguard opened the door. I hid behind a bush and watched him shake his head at Sheila. Sheila's shoulders raised as she huffed in annoyance, and then she stomped back my way. I flattened myself to the ground under the bush and with a racing heart pounding in my ears, I waited until she'd walked by me to climb out of the undergrowth.

As I stood, a shadow loomed over me.

The bodyguard glared at me.

"Oh, sorry, I dropped my key." I lifted my bungalow key. "See I found it."

"Woman," he grunted the word. "Conrad wants to see you."

"Right. Okay. Sure," I stammered.

Was he about to have me fired? Tell me to leave the island. So many thoughts whirred in my head. The bodyguard eased open the door and waved me inside, then closed it with him on the outside. My heart raced like a frightened bunny.

"Hello?" I called into the semi-dark interior since he had all the blinds closed and only a small amount of light filtered in through the gaps.

"Back here," Conrad's voice echoed through the quiet interior.

His bungalow was the same layout as mine, so I walked toward the bedroom and peeked my head around the door.

"I wanted to apologize," I said, not stepping into the room.

"What for?" he sat up in bed and placed the stack of papers he'd been reading on the side table where a light shone and lit up his face. His skin was still a blotchy pink around his mouth, but he looked so much better than the last time I'd seen him.

I inched around the door. "It's my fault you're in bed injured and missed filming today."

He patted the bed. "You weren't to know."

I stepped closer and folded my arms. "If I'd known, then I wouldn't have kissed you."

"Is that right?" He kicked the sheets aside and stood.

"What are you doing?" I rushed forward and shoved his bare chest. "You should be in bed. You almost died."

As he staggered backward, he captured my hands with his and tumbled us onto the bed, laughing the entire time.

"I didn't almost die," he said beneath me.

"It seemed like you did to me."

He lifted a hand and brushed my crazy hair back. "I love your hair. What is your name, wild woman?"

"Natalie." I swallowed. "Natalie Katz. Please don't have me fired from the film."

"You're an actress in the movie?"

"It's my first movie role," I squeaked out.

He rolled over, so he was on top of me. "Welcome to the film world."

"Some welcome." I frowned.

"Very memorable, if you ask me."

"I'd prefer to remember my first film another way."

He rose an eyebrow. "Have you eaten shellfish today?"

"No. Why?"

His lips were on mine in less than a second. I kissed him back, so grateful he wasn't holding a grudge against me. If anything, he held a growing erection against me. I sighed into his mouth, letting his tongue stroke mine. Soon, the kiss grew desperate. My palms stroked his bare back, my mind recalling the tattoo I wanted to trace with my tongue. I shoved him off me, gasping for air.

"Sorry. Too fast?" he asked.

I shook my head. "Too slow."

Sitting up, I ripped my top over my head and threw it on the floor. Conrad's eyes darkened to lust-filled globes. Then he took over my undressing and stripped me of my skirt and panties. I kicked off my shoes and lay naked at his mercy.

"I want you," I said. "But don't think I'm doing this for any other reason other than you're hot and I have a thing for bad boys who take what they want."

He chuckled. "I'm attracted to wild girls who almost kill me."

"You like to live dangerously?"

"Always." He lowered his head to my stomach and swirled his tongue around my belly button. "When I stopped you from falling over the gangplank, I knew you were trouble. I love trouble."

"And here I believed you didn't take notice of me."

"Oh, I took notice." He circled his tongue on my hipbone.

My body jerked and my legs opened in a natural invitation for him to keep going with his tongue.

"I noted the little dress you wore hanging off one shoulder, begging me to trace your skin with my lips."

I ran my finger over my shoulder. "This one?"

He caught my hand in his and swept my fingers to his mouth. Then he rose above me and kissed my shoulder. His lips glided soft kisses over the sensitive skin. Soft moans spilled from my mouth as I understood his fascination with shoulders.

"Should you be using your mouth so much?" I asked, dimly aware of a reason we shouldn't be doing this.

"Would you prefer I didn't?" He trailed kisses to my other shoulder.

I swear the spot was a direct turn-on to my core that was clenched in need.

"Nope. Keep going." I opened my legs and hooked them around his waist.

"One second." He sat back and opened the bedside drawer, took out a foil packet, and rolled on the condom.

If I was going to say no, this was the time to do it, but yes reverberated through my head and my body. Conrad shifted back between my legs and stared at the junction of my thighs.

"Can I touch you?"

"Please," I begged.

He slid his hand between us and found my slick arousal. His fingers glided over me with ease, heightening my lust until I couldn't take his teasing any longer.

"I need you inside me now."

"How do you want me, wild thing?"

"Rough and fast." I glanced around the room. "The chair there."

His answering grin made more arousal drip between my legs. He must have experienced it because he thrust two fingers inside me hard and fast, like I wanted his cock.

"Conrad." I gasped and grabbed his wrist. "Don't make me come yet."

"You're so close."

"Yes." I panted and writhed against his hand.

Each thrust of his fingers stroked my insides into a tightening of inner muscles, and each brush over my sensitive clit made my legs shake. I was so close to orgasm. My eyes slammed shut, so I'd focus on the sensations building in my body. Conrad stopped thrusting and held his fingers deep inside me.

"I've wanted no one as much as I crave you," he said.

My eyes flew open and met his heated gaze. He drew his fingers out, sending ripples through my body, then he caught my hands in his and hauled me out of the bed toward the chair.

"You want me here?"

I nodded. "Sit."

He followed my request and sat on the chair. I took him in my hand and stroked the condom-covered length.

"Your turn to tease?"

I smirked and nodded, but each slide of my hand made me think about how he'd feel inside me, so I inched forward, spread my legs, and guided his cock into my welcoming slickness. I sat down, joining us as deep as he could go. The best pleasure I'd ever had. He was large. Thicker than any man I'd ever been with before, and I experienced a pleasurable stretch with his size. Our lips met in a hungry kiss. His hands caught my hips in a bruising hold and rolled me on his cock. I took over and lifted my hips and rode him fast the way I wanted. Our mouths broke apart at the furious pace, but he placed his mouth on my shoulder and nuzzled the skin. Shivers of desire raced down to my clit like he'd stroked me there.

"Harder." I moaned.

He suckled my skin into his mouth harder until each tug of his mouth felt like he sucked my clit. Still, I rode him. His cock slid along my insides, hitting all the right places. I wound tighter. My legs quivered and struggled to keep pace as my orgasm raced to the surface. Conrad's hands took over, pumping my body up and down his hard length until I shattered into a thousand lustful, brilliant sparkling pieces of ecstasy. He fucked me through my orgasm before lifting his mouth from my shoulder, capturing my lips with his again, and coming inside me with a sexy groan as he ejaculated loudly.

Our kiss turned softer, more tender as though now we'd sated our lust, we settled into being cuddle bunnies. His hands stroked my body as my hands stroked his. For a long time, we traced each other's curves and hollows. Our tongues spoke a language of intimacy neither of us possessed with each other, but the kiss felt like the beginning of something special.

He stood, carrying me in his arms, and said, "Stay the night."

"I'm not sure."

He placed me on the bed. "I wasn't asking."

A grin formed on my lips as I placed my arms behind my head and settled back on the pillow. "I wasn't intending to go anywhere."

"Are you going all clinger stage ten on me?"

I bit my lip. "I'll go if you want me to."

He laid his head on my stomach. "I want you to stay. I was joking."

"Tell me something."

"What?" He rolled over and placed his head on the pillow.

I rolled over, so we were face to face. "Why doesn't everyone know you're allergic to shellfish?"

He sighed. "I had a stalker who was obsessed with me."

"The definition of a stalker."

"Shush." He kissed me. "Anyway, when I didn't return her affection, she broke into my apartment and put shellfish in every food in my fridge. After the incident, my publicist concluded it'd be best to keep my weakness away from the public."

I kissed his cheek. "I'm sorry you experienced that. Are you in danger when you're famous? I've always dreamed of being a famous actress."

"It's not serious. I love it. There are some bad things, but the good far outweighs the bad."

"Tell me more about you."

"What do you want to know? I have an awesome brother, Tate. He's an actor too."

"Everyone knows your brother. Tell me about you. What do you like? Favorite food? Those sorts of things."

"All right, but only if you tell me yours."

"Deal."

He placed his arm over my body and stroked my shoulder. I wrapped my arm around his waist and traced his back knowing there was a tattoo under my fingers waiting for me to explore. As we gazed into each other's eyes and revealed more about ourselves than I ever had with a man, I couldn't help but wonder if this was a onetime thing, a film location hookup, or the beginning of more.

Six weeks later, the director yelled, "That's a wrap, everyone."

Cheers exploded from the cast. I clapped with them. Even though my part was small, they'd contracted me for two weeks of filming, because Conrad's allergic reaction forced them to reschedule the shooting. So I ended up staying the entire six weeks of filming on the island. Which meant more time with Conrad. I'd steal across to his bungalow every night where, after a long day of filming and not being able to touch each other, we'd pounce, have wild sex, then snuggle in his bed sharing parts of our lives.

To say I was smitten was an understatement, but I was also a realist. Our lives were about to go their separate ways. Him to his superstar life and me back to acting in commercials. My agent had lined up a role for a beauty product line, which wasn't a terrible thing, as lots of famous actresses did those. Except I wasn't famous yet and my agent had failed to get me another movie role.

It looked like my dream wasn't about to come true yet.

"Hey," Conrad whispered, sidling up to me in the tent while the director continued talking.

"Hi," I whispered.

"You're coming over tonight."

"I should pack."

Even though it'd take me ten minutes to pack, leaving the island and our romance behind was more painful than leaving my dream of being famous.

"Okay. I'll come and help you pack." He strode away.

I stared after his retreating form. Under the shirt he wore, I'd traced the lines of his tattoo many times with my fingers and tongue. Each time was like an exploration of lust and love.

Damn it. I'd fallen in love with the man.

I chatted with the cast, someone popped the cork on a champagne bottle, and we all drank, and I fluttered around the tent wishing this was my life forever. More importantly, wishing Conrad would be in my life forever.

As the champagne stopped, so did the partying, and we all made our way to the bungalows for our last night on the island. The air was so crisp and clean here that each inhale almost washed away my melancholy. I ducked inside the bungalow and flicked on the light, letting out a startled gasp when I spotted Conrad standing inside with a pink rabbit soft toy in his hand.

"What are you holding?"

"A bunny. I got it for you."

I took the soft toy and hugged it to my chest. "It's fluffy. Thank you."

He smiled, then grimaced.

"It's all right," I said. "I understand this is the end of us. You'll go back to your life of the rich and famous and I'll go back to mine."

"Natalie." He sighed.

My bottom lip trembled.

"Don't cry. Where's my wild thing?"

I sniffed back the tears. "I'm here. It's..." A spark of an idea hit. One to cling to, even if it would only be one more night in the future. "Will you come to my Halloween party? I have one every year."

"I'd love to." He tilted my chin up with his finger and stared into my eyes. "I don't want this to be the end."

"You don't?"

"No, my crazy little lust bunny."

"Lust bunny?"

"We met on Easter weekend, remember?"

"Is that why you got me the bunny?" I giggled. "I'd forgotten what with me almost killing you and all."

He grinned. "How could I forget?"

"I'll never forget you and these last few weeks. I was living my dream here with you."

"Keep living it then. Be my girlfriend."

"But?"

"But what? I've fallen for you."

"You have? I've fallen in love with you, too."

"See," he said, drawing me into his firm body. "What's there to argue?"

"Work. I also have two roommates."

He kissed me, silencing my doubts. His lips stroked mine into a heated frenzy, then roamed down my neck to nuzzle on my shoulder. Even since his fascination and now my immense pleasure with shoulders, I always wore an off-the-shoulder top.

"Move in with me. I'll find you work too, or more precisely, my agent will when he takes you on as a client. He noticed you working on the film, and he's already sent an offer to your agent to take over your contract."

"He what?" I sucked in a deep breath, trying to calm the sudden racing in my heart. "You didn't do this, did you?"

"Me?" He shook his head. "He traveled to the island to go over a contract for another film. I had nothing to do with him noticing you. That was all your talent."

I stepped out of his arms and paced the room. Was this real? Was I about to have my dreams come true? They were already halfway there with Conrad in my life, but being a famous actress was my ultimate dream. One I'd worked toward for as long as I'd watched television. Back and forth, I paced. I sensed Conrad's uneasy stare while he gazed at me. I paused and cuddled the bunny again. No man had ever given me a soft toy to remember our meeting. Conrad might be a bad boy, but he owned a squishy heart. His heart was all mine for the taking.

I wanted it.

So much so that I turned and ran, launching myself into his arms and wrapping my legs around him. He caught me with ease laughing as he spun us around in a circle until my head flung back and my wild curly hair flew everywhere.

When he stopped spinning and put me back on my feet, I clutched his shirt in my fists, trying to keep myself upright. His powerful arms steadied me, supported me, and I sensed without a doubt Conrad Saint James was the man destined for me.

"Yes," was all I said.

It was all I needed to say.

Read Olive and Tate's story in The Lustful Leprechaun the third book in the Hollywood Hearts series.

Coming soon Emily and Jake's story in Lustman to the Rescue.

Afterword

Thank you so much for reading The Lust
Bunny.
Did you love my story?
Review it!

A READER WHO WRITES a review for a book
is a tremendous gift to the author. It lets
me know that someone read my book and

enjoyed the story enough to tell me. If you enjoyed this book, please leave a review on Amazon or GoodReads. I'd be forever grateful.

Acknowledgments

First, thank you to my family for putting up with me disappearing into the world of books. To Belinda, thank you for encouraging me to write again after I lost everything in a computer crash. Remember to back up! A lot of work goes into creating a story, and I'm always thankful for the support of my online writing buddies, beta readers, and fellow authors, Immy for always making me smile, Tammy for believing in me from the start, Karen for being willing to read any level of heat I write. Cassie for her hand holding. Lana for her invaluable knowledge. Also, my fabulous beta reader Erica and her help with US English. The biggest thank you goes to my 'twin' Dannielle, who is the best critique partner, cheerleader, and sounding board ever, and is forever fixing my comma errors, sorry Dannielle I'm afraid you're stuck with them and me. Finally thank you to all you romance readers. You are my tribe.

About Author

Helen Walton is a tea drinking, chocoholic, romance writer. Stories are her obsession. She adores creating sensual romances containing a sprinkling of humor and the all-important happy ending. She lives in South Australia with her family, and menagerie of quirky animals where they all take her away from her book world and demand to be fed. Lucky for them, she enjoys cooking but prefers baking.

Sign up for my newsletter for exclusive content.

https://www.helenwaltonauthor.com/newsletter
Visit my website

https://www.helenwaltonauthor.com/

Follow me

𝕒 amazon.com/author/helenwalton

BB bookbub.com/profile/helen-walton

f facebook.com/Helen-Walton-Author-1034966677 06602/

g goodreads.com/author/show/20249188.Helen_W alton

📷 instagram.com/helen.walton.author

𝓟 pinterest.com.au/HelenWaltonAuthor/boards/

♪ tiktok.com/ZSJgrfgrC/

HELEN WALTON

Also By

FANTASY AND PARANORMAL ROMANCE
Summer Court

Fae's Song

Fae's Wolf

Fae's Alpha

Fae's Heart

CONTEMPORARY ROMANCE
Billionaires' Reluctant Brides

Their Love Deal

His Pleasure Contract

Love Negotiations

Her Love Submission

Hollywood Hearts Short Stories

How The Grinch Lusted After Santa

Lusting After Valentine

The Lustful Leprechaun

The Lust Bunny

Anthologies

Reluctant Bride

Alpha Male

www.ingramcontent.com/pod-product-compliance
Lightning Source LLC
Chambersburg PA
CBHW030418120726
47904CB00007B/2335